HIS DIRTY SECRET 9

SIDE CHICK CONFESSIONS BOOK 9

MIA BLACK

Jayla

Damiah was gone. She walked away so fast and as soon as she hit the corner, she disappeared, but she left all her bullshit behind with me. How the fuck did she find me again? And why the fuck was she still talking about Shane? I thought he said he had it all handled, but by the way she was talking, it sounded like he was handling more than what he was telling me. Was he really still fucking her? Or was she just messing with my head? And here I was in a place that I didn't want to be. Now I was knee deep in some fucking drama.

I went inside my house after telling my

neighbors that I was fine over and over again. They looked at me shocked and shook their heads. I guess they'd never seen me like that or maybe they never seen a situation like that before, but that bitch was fucking crazy. She was pushing me to my limit and I had to put her in check. She really thought that she could just come up in my face and I was going to do nothing. I smiled at my neighbors to try to make them feel better before I went home and closed my front door. Once I was settled inside, I locked all the doors and closed up all the windows. I knew Keon could be home any minute, and we're so used to leaving the door unlocked sometimes, but with that crazy bitch Damiah, I was not taking any chances. For all I knew, she could wait till this whole shit died down and pop up in my fucking house. I didn't have time for that bullshit either.

This shit got me all types of fucked up. I had to get to Shane and talk about this. I would call him now, but I was not in the right place or frame of mind to talk. I was so pissed off, who knew what I would say? I couldn't even get my mind to stop racing so I knew I wouldn't say the right words. Despite all of this shit, I still liked Shane and before I went popping off on him, I needed to cool down.

My bottle of pinot grigio was screaming for me. Thank God Samara gave me some extra bottles of wine from her wine of the month club. Right now, I just needed to vibe out. I poured a huge glass of wine and started blasting some Solange. This was the time that I needed to have "A Seat at the Table." I hummed along sipping the wine and made my way to the bathroom. By the time Solange was hitting the high notes in "Cranes in the Sky," I was running the water for my bath. I put in the best bubble bath and added some oil for my skin. The lights were dimmed low and I even lit a few candles. I really needed to feel chill.

The second my body hit the warm bubble bath, I felt relaxed, if not for a little bit. Bobbing my head to "Lovers in the Parking Lot" and taking the final sip of my glass of wine, I was trying to push the memory of what happened earlier out of my head. The music and the wine were helping but it wasn't enough. It was crazy to think of how Damiah just popped up here. That bitch is really crazy. All this over Shane?

I felt my eyes get watery, but I blinked the tears away. The last thing I needed was to be crying over this shit. I thought I was done crying over a man. I thought I was done crying over fucking drama. I just couldn't believe my luck. I left Atlanta to come to Houston to run away from all the tragedy. I was here to leave Darius and his married man bullshit behind. Haunted by the fact that he died in my arms, I was done with all that shit, but now, Samara's brother Shane, had changed all of that. Now, he was all that I could think about. Now, I couldn't get over him. Now, I just wanted to picture my life with him. And now, I was knee deep in some bull-shit because of him.

What if Damiah was telling the truth? What if she really was fucking Shane almost every night? I didn't want to believe it, but I didn't want to think the last guy I was with was married either. One second I was falling for Darius and the next he was married to some crazy bitch. What if Damiah was crazier than Shanice, Darius' wife? Shit, she might be.

Shanice didn't come for me, she went straight for Darius and look what happened...he was dead. How crazy was Damiah? And if she was telling the truth...was I a mistress all over again?

CHAPTER 1

Trell

I didn't want to, but I almost couldn't help myself. All it took was for me to think about it and I had to do some research. Fucking Shane! It was bad enough that he has the woman of my dreams wrapped around his finger, but now his face was everywhere. I was online and I saw an ad for his gym. I was scrolling around looking at another one of his gyms and shit. How many of these gyms did he have? It's like just when one of those gyms opened up, another one popped up out of nowhere. Who the fuck does he thinks he is? Does he think he's like fucking McDonald's or something? Fucking piece of shit. He was the reason that I was unhappy. Because of him, I'd never get to be with Damiah.

I met Damiah years ago and she was so cool. She had this way about her and I could see even back then that Shane didn't appreciate her. He would take her to places, but after some time, he started treating her like some sort of groupie bitch. He started to act like she was a chick that he met after he started making money. I didn't want to feel sorry for her, but it was hard not to. Damiah was beautiful but you think Shane saw that shit? Nope. He was too busy with some other shit to know that he got a good woman; a fucking ride-or-die chick. Damiah that type of chick that will hold you down and have your back, but Shane was too stupid to see that shit.

Something happened years ago that made Shane change. Something in him just shifted and I noticed it early, but I played it off. I didn't want to think that about Shane. I thought maybe I was being paranoid, or even maybe I was too busy looking at Damiah and not at Shane. But time went on and I could see him pulling away from me, the business,

and Damiah. Shit changed and this motherfucker left and dipped. He did me dirty and
fucked up Damiah too. One of these days I'd
get even. One of these days...

My phone vibrated and I was going to
ignore it, but when I saw the name and
number, I was surprised. Shit, I had to blink
hard to make sure it was the right person.

"What are you doing calling my phone?
You misdialed or some shit?" I tried not to
smile but I couldn't help it.

"What's that supposed to mean?"

"You know exactly what that means." I
chuckled. " Don't try to play. It's not like you
call me every day. Shit, you don't even call me
every once in the while." I laughed.

"Well maybe things will change. I might
start calling you more often nigga. Stop acting
like you not looking forward to my phone
call." She laughed.

"What's going on Damiah?"

Damiah has always had my number, but
she never really called me. Back in the day
when she called me, it was because she had
some message from Shane. We were friends in
a way, so sometimes she would call me, but

that wasn't all the time. It was still weird to see her number though.

"I just needed to talk," she said and I had to stop myself from laughing.

"Just to talk?" I shook my head. I could tell when she was up to something. Or if something was wrong with her. "What's up Damiah?"

"What?" She was trying to sound innocent.

"Stop playing. Yo, this is me you're talking to. So stop trying to hold back and tell me what's really going on."

"Can I come over?"

I stood up when I heard that. I couldn't think of the last time me and her really hung out. It's been a minute and we never really hung around each other alone.

"Yeah, it's cool. You know where I live?" I asked but of course she knew.

"How could I forget?" She laughed and I did too.

After the phone call ended, I got up and started walking around my home. I looked out the window at my huge yard. It was a lot of land and a huge pool that I got done after I saw the same one on this reality show. It was so fucking huge and the guy that owned it was a real estate millionaire. His whole place looked like a museum. Once I saw that show, I started to think differently. Shit, I was a millionaire too but I made my money in another way, but that didn't mean that I couldn't get nice shit too. So after watching that show, I went and got the latest cars, nice ass clothes, and this huge fucking mansion.

The first time I saw this mansion, the shit looked haunted. It was covered with vines and leaves and all types of craziness. It looked like it should have been torn down, and when I purchased it, niggas were looking at me like I was crazy. They didn't see what I saw. They were too busy looking at all the work I had to do, but they missed the big point. They didn't see that the house was far away in a closed off community. The neighborhood was dead and there was only one road to get here. I could see who was coming in and who was coming out. So after I fixed the house up, I built another little house by the end of the road so that my niggas could keep a lookout. I even set up cameras; I was taking no chances on nothing. When everything was done, I was happy with what I had.

My phone was vibrating again and I saw that it was one of my workers.

"What's up?" I asked him.

"I got some chick here named Damiah saying that she's here to see you," he informed me.

"It's cool."

Minutes later Damiah was at my door. I looked at her and she was even more beautiful than the last time I saw her. She had her hair down and was wearing a green dress that matched her eyes. I remember when I first met her and I wondered if her eyes were real. So many times chicks like to wear colored contacts and pretend that it's theirs. But the more that I hung around Damiah, I figured out that the color of her eyes were real and that she was a real ass chick too.

"How you doing Trell?" She smiled at me. She stood in front of me and started to look at me weird.

"What's up? Why you looking at me like that?"

"I'm wondering what's up with you. You

the one that is acting funny." She opened her arms up. "Where's my hug?'

"Oh, we hug now?" I chuckled. I hugged her and almost grabbed her ass, but I didn't. "What you want from me?" I looked down at her.

"I can't hug you without wanting something?" She was giving me that playful smile; that's when I knew something was up.

"You act like we hug all the time. Damn, to be honest we barely talk all the time."

"But that doesn't mean we're not friends, are we?" She gave me a slick smile. "Come on Trell, be nice to me. I just need someone to talk to right now."

"Let me guess, it's about Shane." I figured that's what she was here for. It was always about Shane.

"Ehhhh...." She sighed. "Let's not get into all that just yet."

"Not yet?" I didn't understand what she meant but when I looked at her face. I could tell she really didn't want to talk about it. "Okay, so what are we going to do?"

"Hmm, let's just talk about my day."

I walked her to my living room and sat

her down on my couch. I asked if she wanted anything to drink and she just wanted water. While I went to get her a bottle of water, she started to talk about the hair salon where she worked. She'd been there for a minute and everyone that I knew that got their hair done by her liked her a lot. The ladies kept talking about how she was the best stylist in the shop. She had skills and I wondered why she never had her own salon.

"So, this lady came into the salon with a picture of Beyoncé with some long blonde weave in her hand. She handed me the picture and was like she wanted to look just like the picture."

"So she wanted to look like Beyoncé? Just like Beyoncé?" I asked and she nodded. "Was she even close to looking like her?"

"The bitch couldn't even look like her shadow. She was just...." She shook her head. "You know what, I'm not even going to in and clown her ass. I'm just going to say that, she looked nothing like Beyoncé. Anyway she still had this long blonde weave and she didn't even have two inches of hair to work with. I mean how was I going to stitch the weave on to her head?"

"So you gave her a wig?" I shrugged my shoulders. I was done talking about hair but it made Damiah feel better, so I kept forcing myself to talk about it some more.

"No, I gave her a full head weave."

"I honestly don't know the difference." I chuckled.

"Then let's just say that I hooked her up! She looked so good and she brought back two of her girlfriends. Now that I did all three of them I now have three regular clients."

"That's what's up. You always was like a magician when it came to the hair. I wonder why you don't have your own salon? You got clients out the ass so it's not like you are going to be starving for money. You should do your own shit."

"Do you know how much of a headache that is? I have to hire people and pay for electricity and shit. All that adds up and I don't even know if it's worth all that. I like the fact that I can rent my little booth and stack up my paper. I make more money in my chair and I don't have to worry about paying rent for the salon. I don't have to worry about paying people and all that technical shit. Let me just do my hair and keep my coins."

"I didn't even look at it that way, smart girl. You always was about the paper."

"Only broke bitches don't care about paper!'

The day went on and somehow we ended up watching TV together. We were watching Netflix shows on the big screen and she was hogging the remote. We started watching movies but then we got into shows. She was watching that ratchet reality shows that some females love to watch.

"Damn girl, how many episodes of this prison drama shit you going to watch?" I asked.

"It's a good show." She looked at me. "That white girl is so bougie and she don't even know it." She pointed at the blond. "And you see that Hispanic girl with the fat ass and thick thighs?" I nodded. "She's fucking the guard and she's pregnant with his baby."

"Okay."

"She's so dumb though because if I was in her shoes, I would have that shit planned out."

"What you mean? How would you plan that shit out? These bitches are in prison."

"Look, they thinking so small, but my ass would have been had it all figured out. The second I found out that I was pregnant with the guard's baby, I would have told him to start looking for work in another prison or state." She paused. "Nah, it would have to be another state so that people wouldn't find out as easy. I would have started looking into technical schools and shit in that state. Then 9 months later down the line, when the baby came out, he would have been in a new state and had the baby in daycare or whatnot. After that I would have got out and got into school and busted my ass a good student. By the time the baby is 5, I would have a job and be with my man. We wouldn't be worried about me finding work because I did all the research while I was in prison. These bitches don't think like that. They too busy sucking dick to think ahead." She laughed.

I shook my head. This chick was smart as fuck but I bet Shane's ass never let her know that. Fucking piece of shit. How could he not see what he had?

"That's smart," I told her. "You're really smart Damiah, you know that?" I looked at her.

"Of course I know that," she replied in a playful tone.

"Nah I'm dead serious. You really are smart." I looked her right in the eyes. "You should know that."

"Thank you." She slid closer to me on the couch. She went back to her prison drama, but she put her legs on top of mine. She smelled so good and felt even better closer to me. I smirked at her and she smiled back.

"You want something else to drink?" I asked her. "Or are you going to want another water?"

"What else you got?"

"Come on, you know I got a little bit of everything."

"I keep forgetting you got like a whole liquor store in here." She got up and walked towards the kitchen. I watched her ass sway back and forth. I wanted to smack it real quick, but I kept my hands to myself even though she wasn't making it easy.

My kitchen was huge and I had a whole

section just for liquor. I had a bunch of beers, wines, brown liquor, clear liquor, and etc. In my other safehouses I didn't have as much, but home I made sure I was stocked up on liquor.

"It's like a store." She laughed. "It feels like you should have a shopping cart or basket when you're in here."

"You want to take some home?" I chuckled. "It's going to cost you."

"Oh please, you would never make me pay." She winked at me. She was right.

After mixing a whole bunch of shit together, we went back to the couch to watch her prison drama again. We were sipping watching these prisoners go through some bullshit. The last thing I wanted to do was watch anything about prison because of my past, but I let that shit slide because of Damiah. She was really into the show, but that didn't stop her from coming closer to me and being under me. She got so close that we were cuddling at one point. I had my arm around her and she was laying on my chest.

"Okay, I think we're about to get into another season," she said. She took the remote and started to change to the other season.

"Nope, this is where I stop this prison soap opera." I took the remote back. "I've had enough of that prison shit."

"Oh, don't be bitter." She held my face. "The past is the past Trell. You can watch this shit without crying so I think we call that progress." She smiled.

"Whatever yo." I sighed. "We're watching something else."

"Watch what? It better not be some kiddy movie. I'm a mother and I watch enough of that shit at home. I need to watch some adult things. I'm here to watch some grown up shit."

"Like what? Like porn?" I joked and started to laugh.

"Why not?" She looked me right in my eyes.

I stopped laughing and took a gulp of my drink. The way she was looking at me, I knew what she wanted, but I couldn't play these games with Damiah. She either wanted it or she didn't.

"If you want to put it on, go ahead and do that," I told her. "But I don't think you about that life."

"About what life?" She asked but that look she was giving me, I knew she knew what I meant.

"You want to find out?' I reached out and touched her face. She nodded and I leaned in and kissed her.

She pulled my shirt and brought me closer to her. I put her on top of me and she started to move her hips. She circled her hips around and started to dry ride me. My dick got hard so quick and when she felt it, she hopped up and down on it. I leaned back on the sofa and she just knew what to do. She took my dick out and rolled her tongue out and licked the head.

"Shit," I mumbled. She was licking me so slow.

"You want it?" she teased, flicking her tongue at it quickly. She was looking me right in the eyes. She was just so sexy.

"You need me to tell you?" I chuckled. "Nobody ever told you what a hard dick means?"

"I just like to hear it." She sucked the head slowly. "So tell me you want it." She went all the way down and almost took it all in. She started to speed up and I put my hand on the back of her head. I was about to control her, but she stopped.

"What?"

"You never told me that you wanted it."

"Stop with these games Damiah." I smiled and she went back to work. She went faster and I put my hand back on her head. I started to control her head's movements and I felt myself almost get there. Shit felt magical the way she was doing it. She slowed down and took more of me in. Next thing I knew, I emptied all in her mouth.

"Come here." I grabbed her and brought her dress up over her head. She wasn't wearing a bra so I kissed her tits. She moaned and grabbed the back of my head. She tongued me down and I slid my finger inside of her. She took a deep breath and began to bite on my earlobe. I added another finger and she moaned even louder. I leaned over and licked her neck. Pumping my fingers in and out of her, she got so wet. She started breathing real hard and fast. When she started to shake, I moved my fingers even faster inside of her. She started to fall so I let her down on the couch.

"Just fuck me." She was reaching up to me trying to pull me close. I licked my fingers.

"Sweet," I teased her and she was still catching her breath.

"Fuck me," she said and I shook my head.

"Not yet." I smiled as I undressed myself. "I ain't rushing this shit." I got down to my knees and opened her legs. "I'm taking my time so I can enjoy everything."

I licked her lips and opened it up. She tasted even sweeter from the source. She started shaking and twisting around. She couldn't control herself and kept trying to pull away from me. I locked her legs down so she could stop moving around. I moved my head around stronger and faster.

"Fuck!" she screamed. "Damn, I can't take it," she moaned. "It's so good baby. It's so fucking good," she moaned loudly. "Fuck! Fuck!" she yelled loudly and the next thing I knew my face was covered. I gave her two soft pecks again, but she started squirming around.

"Stay still." I was trying to make her splash again. "Let me get some more of this."

"Uh-uh. I can't lie still anymore." She giggled and brought my face up. She kissed me all over. "Now will you fuck me?"

"Are you asking me?" I smirked. She bent over and went on all fours.

"I'm begging Zaddy."

That shit made me rock harder than I ever thought. I slowly put myself into her. She was begging for more, but I just teased her with the head. Pulling my head in and out of her, she was shaking more than she did before. I whirled around my head and put my hand against her back. She felt so soft and I started to slide more inside of her because she was just so wet. I couldn't help it. I just started slamming myself into her. She was screaming and when I heard how wet she was, I went crazier. I went faster and she was yelling out, "Yes!" every time I hit her.

"Damn baby," she moaned. Her body fell a little but I still had a grip on her hips. She then started to throw it back on me and I smirked.

"I thought you was giving up on me." I smacked her ass.

"You think you can fuck me and I can't

have some fun with you?" She turned and gave me a smile. "Come on," she challenged me. "Show me what you got."

We started fucking everywhere. Every time we stopped, we just found a new position. We were in the kitchen and she was standing against the sink while I was behind her putting it back in. She put her head back and leaned against my shoulder. She groaned and hissed as I slid back in her.

"How can it feel so good every time you do that?" she asked but I didn't answer. I was too busy grabbing her tits and pumping in and out of her. She came again and I was about to finish off once more. I was just about to pull out when she pushed up against me more.

"I'm about to—"

"I know, but I don't want you to stop," she told me so I bust inside her and we both fell against the sink breathing hard.

I walked back to the living room. I was dazed about what just happened. I was covered in sweat, so I went to the kitchen sink, turned on the water, and splashed some cold water on my face. Damiah looked at me with a smile and leaned over to rinse her face too.

"And now off to the bedroom." She took my hand and I led her to my bedroom. I fell against the bed and she lied down next to me.

"One more?" I asked her.

"I think we fucked enough." She giggled and I laughed along. "How about we take a break?" She looked over at me and winked. She slid over to me and laid her head against my chest. "Besides, it's time to sleep." She yawned.

The alarm clock next to me bed did say it was now after midnight. Did we fuck for that many hours?

"Oh shit." I chuckled. "I didn't even notice the time. How long were we going at it?" I asked her but when I looked down, she was asleep. I kissed her forehead and smiled. Finally, I got the woman of my dreams right by my side; right where she belonged.

CHAPTER 2

Trell

The delicious smell of bacon was the first thing to hit me. It smelled so good that it woke me right up. I rolled over in bed and saw the empty space next to me. It took me a while, but I started to remember what happened the other day. Me and Damiah was fucking for hours and hours and she fell asleep next to me. I threw on some sweatpants and walked to my kitchen. Damiah was in there whipping it like a chef. She cooked bacon, home fries, biscuits, eggs, and some waffles. I grabbed a forkful of food and shoved it in my mouth. It tasted even better than it smelled.

"Damn, what you cooking all this for? Are we expecting more people?" I laughed. "You know, I forgot I had a waffle iron." I sat down. "What's all this for?" I scooped three strips of bacon.

"You mean to tell me after all that happened last night, you can't use some food for some energy?" She winked. "Besides, I know how your ass loves to eat breakfast food all day."

"How you know that?"

"Come on Trell." She gave me a look, "I know you better than you think. Your ass likes to eat breakfast food all day or eat Chinese food all day."

"Chinese food is bomb." I laughed.

"And if I could cook it like the Chinese people make it, I would have made it for you." She smiled. And I knew that she meant that.

It was nice to wake up to this. Damiah in my kitchen making me breakfast and last night still running through my head. She came next to me and brought me a glass of orange juice. She then set a plate in front of me.

"If you wasn't eating while you were waiting, you would have more food."

"You've made enough." I laughed looking at the feast she put out.

"Whatever." She rolled her eyes.

"Thank you." I smiled.

"You're welcome." Everything was so nice and cool. I always knew that me and Damiah could have it like this. If this was our life every day, we could both be happy. She would be with someone that appreciated her and I would be with the love of my life. It could all be so good.

"So what's up?" I asked her. "What you going to get into today?"

"Ugh." She rolled her eyes. "It's...." She didn't finish.

"What?"

"Just a lot of bullshit going on."

"Like what?

"Shane and this new bitch that he's seeing."

Hearing the name Shane pissed me off. It was the last name I wanted to hear, period. I wanted to wild out, but I had to hold it all inside. I didn't want to ruin the moment because Damiah brought up that bitch ass nigga. It's always about Shane.

"What about Shane?" I ate my food slowly. "What he do now?"

"He's just seeing some thot ass bitch. He thinks that he can just be with this ho or something. She's so fucking basic, Trell. You really need to see her. She doesn't look better than me and she got some bum ass job." She rolled her eyes. "She really thinks she's all that and this dumb ass nigga is falling for it. He's so stupid." She went on and on and I started to drown her out. I really didn't want to hear about Shane, especially after last night, but I had to pretend. While I ate breakfast, I just nodded my head and acted like I was listening, but I really didn't give a fuck.

"That's crazy," I said after I saw she was finished. "Don't even think about that though." She nodded her head and started to eat breakfast. There was a little bit of tension, so I changed the subject. "But you never answered my question." She looked up at me from her plate. "What are you going to do today?"

"Today?" She started blinking like crazy. Just like Damiah knew that I love to eat breakfast food all day, I knew that when Damiah was going to lie, she started blinking like crazy. It was the craziest thing to see. "I'm not going to do much. I'm going to run some errands for the salon. I need some new materials so I'm going to be everywhere really. I don't even know where I'm going to be and where I'm going to end up."

"Oh yeah?" I watched her still blink and acted like I really believed what she was telling me, but I knew it was bullshit.

"Yeah! Like, I need some new…curling irons and stuff. I really need some new combs and clips." She was still blinking like she had something caught in her eye or something. "So I'm going to be really busy today. It's going to be a long day and I'm going to be really busy."

After she finished lying, Damiah started to stuff her mouth with food. She didn't look up at me and she kept eating her food.

"I need to get started on this busy day." She finally looked at me and smiled. She got up and put her plate in the sink. She washed her dish and walked over to me. She kissed me softly on the lips. "I better go." She looked me in my eyes and I just gave her a little smile. I wasn't going to let her know that she was lying. What would be the point?

"Yeah I got a long day too. I'll hit you up when I get the chance." She walked out the kitchen and pretty soon I heard the front door close.

The breakfast was too good so I wasn't going to waste it. Damiah got my heart and everything, but the fact that she got to lie, always made me think twice about her. She didn't need to do all that with me, but I couldn't really concentrate on that. After I finished breakfast, I knew it was time to get back to work. Money wasn't going to just jump in my pockets; I had to go out there and make it. After cleaning up the kitchen, I got focused.

"Yo!" Deshawn answered the phone after the first ring. "What's good?" Deshawn was my right-hand man. We handled the streets and the business together. We made a whole lot of money together and he always had my back. I never had to wonder about him really. The only thing that made me think twice about him was the fact that he was almost always faded. Sometimes I would call him and he would be slurring because he was drinking some shit or something else. He liked to pop pills every now and then. I never cared about that though. That nigga was loyal and when things needed to be done, he did it, and that was all that matters for me.

"Time for the money," I told him. "We got some shit to do."

"Cool."

"Make your way over here so we can get down to business."

I ended the call and walked around the huge mansion. Through the windows I could see the workers I hired making sure that the mansion looked great. On the other end of my property, I could see my street guys kicking back and drinking some beers. Usually I would tell them that we couldn't be out here slipping, but I would let this go for a little while. As much as I hate to admit it, Damiah was still on my mind. It was like she was still in this room and still on my dick. Even though she lied to me about bullshit and I should have been really focused on the money, I was just a little distracted. Damiah and I finally got our chance to be something and she had to bring up that bitch ass nigga's name. When would she see that he was no good for her? In fact, he was never good for her. She was just wasting her time with him. And now she was lying? But why? And about what?

"Trell, Deshawn is here." Someone buzzed me and I signaled for them to let him in. Deshawn walked in looking like the hip hop bodyguard he always did. He was 6'3, long ass dreads, and built like a fucking house. This motherfucker was wide and that was why nobody fucked with him. One look at him and they left him alone.

"What's going on?" I asked him. He came in with a big duffel bag and put it on the table.

"This is the money from the last run. I counted it twice, so it's all there." He walked over to the kitchen and went straight to my fridge. "You don't have any beer?" His voice was already messed up and he smelled like liquor.

"I ain't judging you but you had enough. Plus you always coming here and emptying my fridge. The fuck this place look like to you? A store?"

"But it does look like a store though." He laughed. "Damn, you never complained before. What's going on with you?"

"Nothing is going on with me."

"Nah, you acting different. Let me guess, it's that chick Damiah."

Deshawn knew about me, Damiah, and Shane. I was not shocked that he brought up her name.

"The boys outside said that she was just here." He went on.

"Them niggas need to mind their business and focus on making money."

"Damn what did she do to you?"

"Man, I don't even want to get into all that." I really didn't.

"I don't even know what it is but I know that chick always had your head messed up. Whatever it is, just think straight."

"What you trying to say?"

"I'm saying what I always tell you, leave that chick alone. She fine but she is a lot of trouble."

"It's just her and Shane—"

"And how she's stuck on his ass; man I know. I've heard you tell me this story a thousand times and the shit always ends the same. Listen, we making this money and we got the streets on lock...that's what we need to be focused on. That whole shit with Damiah and whatever she does to you, that's nothing to be thinking about."

Even though Deshawn be leaned out sometimes, he had a point. I was here thinking about Damiah when there was money to be made. Shit, the whole reason that I told Deshawn to come over here was to get to the money, and what the fuck was I doing? Were we even talking about the money? Nah, we here talking about some chick that lied to me for no fucking reason.

"You're right," I told him.

"Yeah I know I'm right. Look, you not no ugly nigga, you got fucking stacks of cash, you got this big fucking mansion," he pointed out. "You don't need to be stuck on no chick. You think she the only bad bitch out there? There are other bad bitches out there that gonna jump on your dick. She ain't the only one out there."

"I get it Deshawn." I sighed. "I already said you right." I chuckled. "You don't have to repeat the shit again."

"Cool, now where the Henny at?" He grinned and I shook my head.

CHAPTER 3

Jayla

The restaurant was beautiful and the food smelled great. It was so romantic with the low flickering lights that came from the candles, but I just wasn't feeling it. I wasn't in a romantic mood at all. Honestly, I wasn't even feeling very happy. Looking across the table, I studied Shane's face and expression. Shane looked like he was doing okay but I could tell that he was nervous, and he should be. The whole shit with his baby mother was hanging over us like a dark cloud. I just coudln't believe that it happened again. He kept avoiding my eyes. I shook my head and crossed my arms.

When the waiter came over, even he could tell that something was up. There was this huge tension between Shane and me. We gave our orders and I asked for two glasses of wine, back-to-back.

"It's a nice restaurant." Shane finally spoke to break the ice. I gave him a look. Was he really going to try to small talk with me? What type of bullshit was he on? I didn't want to talk about shit that didn't matter. I knew he knew what was going on.

"It's okay," I mumbled and then smiled when I saw my two glasses of wine make their way to me. I took one quick gulp and handed the waiter back the empty glass. "Thank you." The waiter's eyes opened wide. Shane cleared his throat.

"So, how's work?"

"It's okay."

"Work is pretty okay for me too."

It became silent. I really had nothing to say. Wait, that was a lie. I had *plenty* to say but I didn't want to start getting loud and crazy in this nice restaurant. I was pissed the fuck off but I was not going to let myself get too angry. The food came and I just barely ate any. I was hungry but I didn't feel like eating. I felt like it was so fake for us to even be in this restaurant. Why did he bring me here?

"I don't know where to start." He took a deep breath. "Is something going on?" he had the nerve to ask. He had to know. I opened my mouth but I didn't say anything. Instead, I nodded my head. I wanted to yell but I kept it in. I just sipped my wine slowly. "I'm sorry if I offended you in any way Jayla. You know that it is never my intention to hurt you. I don't know what I may have done, but I'm sorry." And that was when I lost it.

"Sorry? After everything that happened, that's all you have to say sorry?"

"Jayla-"

"No!" I cut him off. "I told you when we first got together that I didn't want any drama." I shook my head. "And now it seems all we have is drama."

"What are you talking about?"

"Don't play dumb Shane, you know what I'm talking about."

"Honestly I don't."

"Well *honestly* I find it hard to believe that

your baby momma popped up on me *again* and that you don't fucking know."

Shane's eyes opened wide and he instantly looked pissed. Either he was a great fucking actor, or he didn't know.

"What?" he said in a low growl.

"You didn't know," I realized.

"What did you say? Did you just say Damiah popped up on you *again*?" I nodded. "Are you hurt? Did she try to hurt you?"

"No. It looked like she wanted to fight but all we really did was end up screaming at each other."

"Jayla, I'm so sorry-"

"Shane, you are always sorry. I'm so sick and tired of it."

"Jayla I understand—"

"Save all that shit. I don't want to hear it." I felt the anger coming up out of me. It was the wine. That damn second glass was making me tell it all. "I told you the last time that if your babymomma came up to me again, that it was going to be a problem. What the fuck is going on with ya two?"

"Nothing."

"Nothing? That's bullshit! No bitch is

going to fight me over some guy she's not fucking," I snapped. "You must think that I'm fucking stupid. I know you still fucking with your baby momma."

I was fuming but I didn't care. I had the right to be mad. All the stress I was going through, he was lucky I didn't throw the glass of wine in his face.

"I can't believe you said that." He looked shocked.

"The fuck you mean Shane? How can I not think that? She over here popping up like bread out of the fucking toaster. You really going to sit there and tell me that this bitch is fighting me because she's *not* with you?"

"That's exactly what it is."

"Bullshit Shane."

"Jayla—"

"Bull-fucking-shit!"

The waiter came over and asked if we were okay. People were looking at us and that's when I realized that I was louder than I thought. We were now the loud couple in the restaurant that people would stare at.

"Everything is fine," I smiled and said in my sweetest voice. "May I please have some water?" I was trying to be as normal as possible, but I was still mad. The waiter nodded and walked away.

"Jayla, you have to believe me that I knew nothing about what happened with you and Damiah recently." He leaned across the table. "And most importantly, you have to know that there is absolutely nothing going on between me and her. She and I have been over for a long time. I would never disrespect you like that. I know that I have withheld information before, but I'm telling you the truth."

"So if ya two are over, then why is she popping up on me? Why is she coming after me if you guys are so called over?"

"She is just obsessed with me. I've told her a million times that we are over, but it seems that she isn't getting it."

"And what am I supposed to do about it?"

"You have to do nothing Jayla. You've been more than patient with this situation." He took a deep breath. "I'm going to take care of it."

"You said that the last time." I rolled my eyes looking away from him.

"I am going to take care of this Jayla."

"Uh-huh."

"Look at me." His voice was sincere and when I looked into his eyes, it was sincere as well. "I am going to take care of this. I promise you that I am going to take care of it."

Shane's eyes had me glued in. He was just so sexy and fine and I couldn't deny that I still had feelings for him. I kinda wish I didn't. It would be easier to walk away from all this drama if I felt nothing for him, but that wasn't the case. I moved all this way to Houston to be drama free and because of Shane, I was back at it again.

"You're lucky you're cute," I joked, shaking my head.

"What?" He laughed. "Are you trying to say that if I was ugly that you would have left?"

"No, not at all." I gave him a slick smile.

"You are something else."

The rest of the dinner went surprisingly well. He kept telling me how beautiful I looked. He was saying it over and over again that I had finally had to ask him about it.

"Why do you keep saying I'm beautiful?"

"Is that a problem?"

"It's not a problem," I started smiling. "I'm just wondering, why do you keep saying it?" I bit my bottom lip. "What are you trying to get at?"

"I'm not getting at nothing."

"Really?" I leaned over the table. "I thought you were having flashbacks of that night." I gave him a knowing look.

"Jayla," he chuckled. "I always have flashbacks."

We flirted the rest of night. It's crazy how the whole dinner took a turn. At first it started with tension because I was so mad, but now we just had this chemistry between us. When we left the restaurant, he pulled me in close and kissed me. It was different this time. His hand was on the small of my back and he pulled me in. Everything about this man felt so damn good. When he slid his hand down to grab my ass, I had to pull away.

"What's up?" he asked. He looked into my eyes and I felt my knees wobble.

"I got work in the morning." I was telling the truth, but it wasn't the real reason. I wanted him so bad, but I knew that having sex with him would only cloud my judgement. As much as I wanted to--and I really wanted to--I just had to back away.

"I understand." He was still holding on to me. "Does that mean that I have to let you go? Do I have your permission to hold on to you for a little bit longer?" His lips were back on mine. He pulled me in closer and I wrapped my arms around his neck. I could feel myself giving in. When my whole body started screaming for him, I let him go.

"I think it's time for me to go home."

He dropped me off at my house and before I went in we kissed again. I looped my fingers with his and held on tight. I was starting to give in to that feeling of wanting to be with him, but I knew it wouldn't be smart...at least not right now

"Let's not...." I sighed. "I have work in the morning." I repeated my pitiful excuse. Inside of me was screaming for Shane, but I couldn't go there; not right away. A part of me still had to cool down after everything that happened with his baby momma.

"I understand." He gave me a grin and then softly kissed my forehead. "If you have to work, you have to work. I'll talk to you later."

CHAPTER 4

Jayla

It was Sunday brunch at my house. Crystal was making the pancakes while I handled the bacon. Keon was at the grocery store getting the orange juice. When we finally gathered at the table, everything looked great. Crystal blessed the food and we just dug in.

"So…" She looked over at me, smiling. "Tell me what's going on with you and Shane? Is it time for me to get fitted for my bridesmaid dress? And you better pick cute colors too. I don't look so good in red. I think that you should get a nice light blue dress and I can wear it with my sexy heels," she joked.

"I wouldn't do that if I were you." I took a deep breath. "Some bullshit is going on."

"What?" Keon asked with his mouth full. "Is he on some stupid shit?" Keon may be my little brother, but he is very protective of me.

"It's not him—"

"Let me guess, it's the baby mother," Crystal interrupted and rolled her eyes.

"Ding! You got it right."

"That chick popped on you again?" Keon asked giving me a side eye. "I don't know Jayla, that shit sounds crazy."

"I know. To be honest, I'm really afraid," I confessed.

"Afraid? Afraid of what?" Crystal asked. "That she's going to fight you again? Why don't you just tell Shane about it?"

"I did, but that's not it. To be honest, it's more than just him. I can't believe…" I drifted off. I felt myself get angry, so I took a deep breath.

"What?" Crystal asked. Keon started to look concerned so there was no way I couldn't tell them now.

"I just want to back out of it."

"Back out of what?" Keon asked.

"This whole thing with Shane. I just want to leave him alone and just go back to doing what I was doing. I might have to end it with him," I confessed.

Both of their mouths dropped open. I've been thinking about leaving Shane for a while. Even though Shane told me that there was nothing going on with him and his baby momma, it was still a lot of drama. Why would any woman put up with this? It's like I was sitting around just waiting for Damiah to do something to me.

"Wait." Crystal took a deep breath. "I thought you said that you had feelings for him? You told me before that you really like him," she questioned me.

"I do. I really do have feelings for Shane."

"So why would you leave Shane? He seems like such a nice guy. He treats you really nice and for the most part, you are really happy to be with him or even around him."

"But he comes with a little bit of drama," Keon added, eating some of the blueberry waffles.

"But everyone comes with drama though."

Crystal rolled her eyes. "No one is clear and free of drama."

"I know that, but this is a lot to deal with for just one guy. I'm just getting cool with the idea he has a kid, but this baby momma… she's just doing the most."

"I know." Keon nodded. "But you do seem so happy with him though."

Hearing Keon mention me being happy made me smile. I knew that he'd seen me go through a lot.

"Yeah Jayla. I don't know if you know this, but you would come in here cheesing and stuff." She giggled. "You'd be on the phone with him smiling like crazy."

"For real." Keon chuckled. "Remember that time he sent her flowers or something? She was smiling like she won the lottery or something." He laughed.

"Stop teasing." I blushed.

"You see!" Crystal beamed. "You really like him!" She nudged me. "So why would you break up with him? Over some chick?"

"Not just any chick, his baby mother. If this was just an ex, then it's whatever…but he's going to be around this crazy ass chick for the rest of his life. I am being honest when is say that I don't think I can handle it."

Keon shook his head.

"Nope," he said.

"What do you mean by that?"

"Sis, you are happy as fuck with this dude. Besides that shit with his baby mother there is nothing else that you don't like about him. Am I right?" I nodded my head. "Then you need to hang on. Is he helping you out? Is he trying to take care of the situation?"

"He told me that he talked to her but she still pops up."

"Shane is going to handle that." My little brother grabbed some orange juice. "Don't even worry about that. He seems like a guy that keeps his word. I know a lot of guys that bullshit and lie; he don't seem like the type," my brother added, and his girlfriend nodded her head to agree.

"But what about all the drama?" I reminded them.

"Like my girl said, everyone has drama. No one is perfect or even has a perfect past. You just can't expect to date someone and think it's going to be cool and breezy."

"I just don't want to end up in the same situation like before," I started to say slowly. A flash of Darius popped up in my mind. "I don't want to end up...hurt."

I said hurt but what I really meant was dead. The image of Darius dying in my arms is something that haunts me. The nightmares may not have come as often as they did but it was there in the back of my head. What if Damiah was crazy enough to do that to me? What if she really hurt me and there was no turning back? I couldn't let that happen to me, especially when I had my younger siblings to take care of and think about. We already lost our parents, and we don't need any more losses. I appreciated what these guys were trying to do and say, and I got it. Shane made me happy and I was pretty sure that I was falling for him, but I didn't want to be end up like Darius. I had to really think if I wanted to continue this relationship.

CHAPTER 5

Shane

The gym was packed full of people. One of our celebrity sponsors was throwing an event here and it really paid off. Everyone was here to get a picture with her. She was worth all the money we were paying her and more. On top of that, we offered discounted memberships to anyone that was there. We were having so many new people sign up that it was ridiculous. I couldn't wait to go to the back and crunch the numbers. This was turning out to be such a huge success.

"Shane, don't forget that you have a conference call coming in from the fitness company regarding new gym equipment," one of my managers told me. I gave her a confused look. "Remember, you wanted to get that new climbing machine? You know, the one you saw on YouTube."

"Damn, I completely forgot about that. Is there a way that we can reschedule it? We are just so busy today."

"I've tried but the number that is on file is not working. Maybe their phone line is down or something," she suggested. "Want me to email them?"

"No, what's done is done. If I gave them my word about this conference call, I have to go through with it. What time is the call?"

"It's going to be in twenty minutes or so," she said, looking at her watch.

"I'll be in my office. Keep an eye out here for me. The event should be finished in about an hour. If the conference call runs that long, just knock lightly on my door and I'll help you out."

"Okay."

I went to my office passing by all the customers. I wanted to stay out a little bit more, but this conference call was very important. I was trying to get exclusive equipment for my gym. By the time I sat down in my office chair, my cell phone was vibrating. It was weird that they would call my personal line, but I did give it to them in case of an emergency. I looked at the caller ID and saw that it was an unknown number.

"Good morning, Shane speaking," I answered as professionally as I could.

"Fuck you!" She screamed at me. "You fucking bitch! You bitch ass nigga! Fuck you! Fuck you!" She kept yelling and going off. I got up and closed my door. I didn't need anybody hearing this right now. Once the door was completely closed, I sat back in my chair. The phone was still there and the cursing was still going on. By the time I picked the phone up again, it was in the middle of a rant.

"Fucking bitch! You fucking bitch! Who the fuck do you think you are? You think—"

"Shut up, Damiah." I said calmly. My fingers started to rub my temples. It was like I was trying to chase away the oncoming headache.

"Who are you talking to Shane? You don't

talk to me like that, especially when you know how you feel about me. You know you want me. You know you need me. Do you really think that you and that basic bitch have any type of future together? I am the mother of your child, so I am with you forever. I was with you when you had nothing. Now you want to be with some gold digging bitch over me? Over your family? Are you serious, Shane?"

"Damiah, you are out of your fucking mind." I grunted into the phone. I looked out my office door and saw that nobody was nearby. I couldn't believe that she was saying this. "It's been such a long time since you and I have been together like that. This shit is over between us. It's done. I will respect you as the mother of my child, but that's it. I'm not going to get back with you...ever."

"That's going to be a problem then."

"It is?"

Yeah, it is." She scoffed. "Because I'm going to come after you if you don't come back to me."

I was silent for a second. I had to really make sure that's what this crazy chick said to me. The headache I was trying to stop from happening showed up anyway.

"What did you just say?" I gritted my teeth.

"You heard me," she said in that sarcastic ass tone.

"Don't punk out right now. You was big and bad when you said the first time." I told her. "So be big and bad *again* and tell it to me *again.*"

"I said," she snapped, "if you don't come back to me, I'm going to get you."

"I thought that's what your dumb ass said."

Damiah had lost her mind. She was beyond control. Who was this chick and what happened to the one that I met all those years ago? It was like there were two different versions of Damiah. There was the woman that I was in love with back in the day and this crazy ass chick.

"Damiah, what are you doing? Just what the fuck do you think that you're doing? What the fuck are you even saying right now? Do you fucking hear yourself when you speak?" I snapped but was trying to keep calm. I had a gym full of customers and I didn't need them to hear none of this bullshit.

"I'm not doing anything but being your baby mother for the rest of your life. What you and I have is forever. You stupid to think that you and that basic bitch will last. She is just a thot that you will fuck and get out of your system. She is going to be a memory like those other chicks you use to fuck around with. So just get rid of her."

"Damiah—" I started but she cut me off.

"And you will never get over me. You think you will, but you won't."

"Damiah—"

"You love me Shane and you will always love me. You know that and I don't understand why you act like you don't."

"Damiah…" The headache was making me lose my patience and she kept going on and on.

"What?"

"I'm never leaving Jayla," I informed her.

Damiah started cursing me out worse than before. She just kept going on and on and there was no way of stopping her.

"What did you just say?"

"Is something wrong with my son?" I asked out of nowhere, completely changing the subject.

"No, why would you say that?"

"Because if this is not about our son, then you need to get the fuck off my line with this bullshit. If this is not about our son, then you don't even need to be calling me. If this is not about our son, then you need to stop. Damiah, you're not my girl, you are only my son's mother. Get that shit through your thick fucking skull. I promise you that when you do, it will be much better. When you finally get that, you can live your life and let this thing that you think we have go."

"Hmm, that's what you think."

"No Damiah, that's what I know."

"Let's see if that's what happens."

Her tone was slick and smart as usual, but this time I felt something else was behind her words. She was trying to say something without really saying it.

"What are you saying Damiah?"

"You hard of hearing Shane? You've been asking me to repeat myself a lot lately."

"No, you've been saying slick shit under

your breath and expect me not to ask any questions. So what are you trying to say?"

"You keep seeing that basic bitch and I will make sure you never see your son again."

Damiah was crazy but even for her to bring up using my son was the last fucking straw. I wanted to scream at her, but I couldn't take the chance that she was serious. As crazy as she was, she might just up and leave with my son and I'd never see him again. I couldn't have that. I loved my son too much to ever lose him over bullshit.

"If you keep seeing that bitch, I'll take your son and I'll do even more than that." She paused waiting for me to respond, but I wasn't going to say nothing. "Keep seeing that basic bitch and something might happen to her."

"Something might happen to her?" I repeated her words back to her. "What are you trying to say? Are you saying that you will hurt her? That you will try to hurt her?"

"Me? I'm not saying that at all. Shit happens every day, Shane. People get hurt every day. Accidents happen every day; that's all I'm saying."

I didn't even bother fighting with her.

Damiah was speaking some more of her stupid shit but my son shouldn't have to suffer because of it. She shouldn't use my son as a pawn to get me back or to hurt me. Her dumb ass just needed to vent. I wouldn't even get at her for all the crazy shit she did to Jayla. I should be talking to her about what she did to Jayla, but I was not even going to bring that up. If I did, that would just be more drama between me and her. This was what Damiah wants. She just wanted the fucking attention from me and she didn't care where and how she got it.

"Damiah, you know that I love my son. You know I'm a good father."

"I know that Shane."

"You know I'm a good father and you would keep my child away from me? Do you know what's that really doing? If you take our son away from me, you are not just hurting me, but you're hurting our son too."

"Oh now he's *our* son, but just a few seconds ago, he was only your son. The way you talk about him, you make it seem like he's your son and only your son."

"He's our son, Damiah, and he will always

be our son. You are right to say that we will be bonded forever because we are his parents and that will never change, but don't you ever threaten me again with that nonsense. Don't you ever say anything about me not seeing my son."

"Shane—"

"And if you come by my girl it's going to be a bad time. Leave her alone and stay away from her. My relationship with her is not any of your business." My anger was slipping and I couldn't contain myself. "You know what can happen. You know who I am. You know what the *fuck* I can do." I took a deep breath so I could collect myself. "Stop trying me Damiah or you will make me tap into that other side of me. We both don't want that."

I hung up before she could say anything else. Then I blocked the number. I was infuriated. Right now I should have been celebrating my success with this gym but I was not. Instead I felt like I was going back to bad habits. I felt like I was becoming my old self. Only Damiah could get me this mad and bring me back to my old ways. I'd done so much and worked so hard to separate myself from that guy I used to be. I had too much success to go back there and Damiah didn't give a fuck about that. It's like she wanted to see that side of me again and to prove that he existed. If she kept playing around, she was going to see him and feel his rage.

My phone went off again and I didn't recognize the number.

"Hello." I was grumpy.

"Yes I'm calling regarding the exercise machines." It was my business call and hearing the voices on the conference call immediately put me back in business mode.

"Good day. I've been awaiting your phone call. Shall we talk numbers?" I jumped in headfirst and put the thoughts of Damiah and her bullshit behind me...for now.

CHAPTER 6

Trell

The money was flying everywhere and the music was bumping. I loved nights like this. I had one of baddest bitches standing in front of me with the fattest ass. She was the prettiest bottle girl out of all of the girls that I have seen here so far. She smiled at me and immediately sat on my lap. I didn't ask her to and she didn't have to ask me if I wanted her to. All the guys around me were hype. They were going crazy seeing how this chick came up to me, but this shit was regular for me. Bitches like this can smell the money off of me. Shit, they can smell it off my whole crew. Everywhere we went you could tell that we all had money. We were in here poppin bottles, throwing stacks, and making money at the same damn time.

We were partying but were moving pills in the club too. We had mollys, ecstasy, and other party pills. If people really wanted to party, we would help them out. This chick had to know this and that was the reason why she was on my lap right now. She liked the niggas that make fast money. Bitches like this didn't keep my interest for long. I tapped her and nudged her away from me so that I could get down to the business.

"So, now that we got the street corners on lock, we can make even more money if we expand the business." I leaned over to Deshawn. "And now we can start going to clubs and getting people to pass out our pills. We can take this shit to fucking Dallas and push these pills. You know how they like to party over there. And I got a connect that can get us some steroids or some shit."

"Why the fuck would we need steroids?"

"Not us nigga, fucking athletes! We start helping them and shit...damn that's money.

Just imagine if we get an athlete that is in the NFL and he wants pills On top of that, athletes like to fucking party too so that's more money for pills. If we get that one professional football player, we gonna be making a lot more money."

"Relax." He smiled. "I can see your brain racing to think about some new shit, but let's fall back with all that shit. We can take care of that another time. We got bad bitches coming up to us wanting to fuck us and you want to talk about money? Look where we at right now."

"Nigga, I will always be talking about money." I laughed. "You starting to talk like a broke dude right now not caring about money."

"I will always care about money but fat asses are important too." Deshawn started busting out laughing even more. "So take the night off from this and get you one of these bad bitches."

Just then some more bottle service girls came into VIP. They brought us even more bottles. They was coming in and we were paying for everything. You could see other girls outside of VIP trying to get in, but if they weren't sexy, they weren't getting in. There was one that was tall brown skin bottle service girl with a nice ass but had these thighs. I didn't know why, but I couldn't stop staring at her thighs. She caught me looking and she came over to me, smiling.

"Here's your bottle." She handed it directly to me.

"This is some nice customer service." I was looking at that ass and thighs. "What's your name?"

"Fatima." She giggled.

"That's a nice name. Come on and sit next to me. You don't have to be scared. I ain't going to bite you."

"I know that, and believe me, I'm not scared." She laughed. "I just have to get back to work. The manager I have today is being a real asshole. I'm not trying to have any headaches because of him."

"That's messed up. Why don't you go tell him that I requested for you to be here?"

"For real?"

"Yeah! That's all part of customer service.

You have to make sure that the customer is happy, right?"

"I do." She nodded.

"Then that's all he needs to know."

"Can you wait for me though?"

"Wait? For how long?"

"Not that long. I'm going to be clocking out soon anyway."

"You getting off work?"

"Yeah I'm going to be done in like ten minutes or so."

"You going to come back and see me, right?"

"Yeah of course." She smiled. "You're my favorite customer here." She winked. She walked away and I watched her and her thighs.

"See, that's what's up. I was about to get worried about you. The way you was acting earlier." Deshawn laughed sitting next to me.

"Huh?" I didn't understand what he was getting at.

"I thought you wasn't talking to any girls because of that chick."

"What chick? The girl that was up on my

lap before? I wasn't feeling that money hungry bitch. You know that's not my type."

"Nah, not that chick. I'm talking about that other chick."

"Who?"

"You know who I'm talking about. I'm talking about what's her name? The chick that popped up at your house the other day"

"You mean Damiah?" I reminded him.

"Yeah her. I thought that she was going to mess with you night."

"What does she have to do with anything?"

"Because ever since the last time you saw her, you've been acting funny. You usually the one that is up in here going in and having fun, grabbing girls for everyone, but you not doing that. You had one bad chick sit on your fucking lap and you turned her away."

"I told you that I was just not feeling her. I didn't want that thirsty ass thot around me. You saw how fast she sat on my fucking lap? I'm not into that shit.'

"Nah, you stuck on Damiah. You need to relax and have fun here."

"You and that relax shit again. You stay saying that shit."

"That's because that's what you need to do. You can worry about the business some other time and leave that Damiah chick alone." He pointed out to club. It was packed with even more people. "Look at this shit. All these motherfuckers are here to have fun, to get pussy, have sex later, to get twisted, and you here stuck on some bitch." He gave me the screw face. "Nigga!" he said in his Kevin Hart voice. "You need to let that shit go and have some fucking fun."

"I hear you."

"You hear me? Now get that chick to come back."

"Shit, I don't want that thot" I shook my head. "That chick with the fat ass and the thighs though was cool. If she come back like she said she would…"

"It don't matter who you get right now." He started looking around the club. "Where those ladies at?" He looked around some more then said, "Oh shit."

"What?" I looked to where he was staring. "Oh shit."

There she was, Damiah. The woman we were just talking about came through the entrance of the club. She was rolling in the place with her best friend. This whole place was packed but she stood out. She had on this light blue dress with silver heels. She had her hair up in a bun and she just looked gorgeous. Fuck! Why did she have to turn up at the club tonight? Deshawn was trying to get this chick out of my mind, now she was here in the club? Shit!

"Don't let her fuck this night up for you." Deshawn said when he saw me staring at her. "Just keep having fun. Don't even pay her any mind. Fuck, don't even look at the bitch."

"Yeah," I replied but I wasn't really listening to him.

"I know what you need," he told me and the next thing I knew one of the bottle service girls came up to me. "Give this man a lap dance." She smiled and acted like she wasn't going to do it. "Don't be shy. He's having a rough day. Make him feel better." He slipped some money in her hand. She looked down at it. She shrugged and sat on my lap.

The woman started moving slowly and

then quickly. She felt so good against me that for a second, I forgot where I was. I held on to her hips and she leaned back against my chest. Her perfume smelled so sexy.

"Can I see you later?" she asked. I looked at her. She was cute. She was light skin with a nice pretty face, but I couldn't really think about her. "So, can I see you later?" she asked again. I was about to speak but from the side of my eye, I could see Damiah. She was moving to the bar. Some guys were coming up to her and you could tell she didn't want to be bothered with them at all. She was rolling her eyes and trying to focus on her drink, but they didn't listen.

"I'll be right back." I got up and started walking to her. I felt someone pull my arm.

"What are you doing?" Deshawn asked me.

"I'm just gonna be right back."

"Come on man. Forget that girl. Don't go over there," he called after me, but I was already off and gone.

Damiah was now trying to reject this other guy, but he kept hounding her. She kept saying it the nice way but this nigga wasn't getting it, so I slid in.

"Hey babe." I came over to hug her. Once she saw it was me, she looked so happy. "I'm so sorry that I took so long for me to get here. The traffic on the way over was crazy, but I'm here." I kissed her cheek. "You not mad at me baby?"

"Nah I'm good boo." She smiled. "You're lucky you're my boyfriend or else I would not be waiting for you. I'm so glad that you're here."

"Of course, where else would I be? If my girl say she wants to go out to the club, that's where I'm going to be." I saw that the guy from before was still there. "Is he bothering you?" I looked at the guy because he still didn't get the message. I was here pretending to be her man, and he still didn't give a fuck

"She can speak for herself," he said to me. Oh, he wanted to be tough guy.

"Really?" I crossed my arms. "Is he bothering you?" I asked Damiah but I looked him dead in his eyes. He tried to act hard but the bitch in him came out real quick. He backed up and walked away from us.

"Oh my God, you saved my life." She hugged me and spoke in my ear. She smelled even better than the last chick and she felt so soft. That quick hug that I had with her brought back some memories of the other night.

"You owe me," I joked, looking her up and down.

"I owe you so much." She had that look in her eyes. She pulled me real close. "Don't you leave me alone. I don't want anymore thirsty niggas crowding my space." She kissed my cheek and stood right next to me. She gave me a devilish look.

"I got you."

Me and her hung out by the bar. She bought me a shot and we just started gulping it down.

"What you doing out here?" She asked me looking me up and down. She had that same look in her eyes. "You here trying to get with some of these ladies?"

"Maybe I am, maybe I'm not. Is that a problem?" I was trying to figure out if she was jealous or just being playful. If she was jealous that meant she felt something too and maybe she finally got bitch ass Shane out of her system.

"Not at all." She grinned at me and I was still confused. What did she want from me?

"So what's up with you?" I looked around the club. "What's up with your friend? Wasn't she here with you? Where did she go?"

"Britanya?" She started looking around the club too. "I don't know. She said she would be back but I ain't seen her since. Who knows? She's probably getting her ass rubbed on by some nigga."

"Ah, you sound jealous. You want your ass rubbed on too?" I grinned.

"Why? Are you saying that you wanna rub my ass?"

"Who knows?" I laughed.

"You touched me like that before and you still want more?"

"Stop acting like you don't want more too." We both started laughing.

A song came on and Damiah jumped off the bar stool.

"We got to dance to this! I love this fucking song!" she screamed, jumping up and down.

"I don't know how to dance to this slow

shit," I complained. "Besides, I don't dance anyway."

"Come on, it's so simple. You just move real slow and hold on to me."

"Oh, that's it?" I looked in her eyes and she started blushing.

"Well there's more." She licked her lips.

"What else?"

"How about you rub on my booty too?"

I didn't even get to answer her before she dragged me out to dance. She put her arms around me and I held on to her waist.

"Don't be scared now," she teased.

"I ain't scared."

"So, why didn't you put your hands on my ass?"

"You telling me to?"

"You're so scared." She slid my hands on her ass. "Better?"

"It's alright," I joked and gave it a squeeze. "It feels nice though."

We moved around slowly and she put her head on my chest. She felt so good and the memories of the other night came running back to my head. I just tried to not think about it, but I couldn't help it. She pulled me in close and lightly kissed my lips. Before we knew it, we were fully making out on the floor. She had a tight hold on me and I was gripping that ass. She pulled away and she gave me a look. It was the same look she gave me when we were at my house that day.

"You want to get out of here?" I asked her. She didn't answer really. She just nodded her head and smiled a little bit. I knew what she meant so I took her hand. We started walking through the club and I looked back to VIP. Deshawn was there and I nodded at him. He saw me with Damiah and shook his head. I shrugged my shoulders and went for the exit.

"Yo," Deshawn said. I looked behind me and he was right there. How the fuck did he get behind me so fast?

"What's up?"

"I got to talk to you." I had a feeling it might be some bullshit, but it could be about the business.

"One second," I told Damiah and walked away with Deshawn.

"What are you doing?" Deshawn asked me as soon as we were away from Damiah.

"Nigga, what does it look like? I'm about

to leave with her. We about to go back to the crib."

"Man, you need to forget this chick."

"How can you say that when I'm about to leave with homegirl right now?"

"You think she really gives a fuck though? She don't give a fuck about leaving with you. She don't even really give a fuck about you."

"Here you go with that preaching shit again. I don't got time for your lectures." I was about to walk back to Damiah, when he stopped me again. "What?"

"Come with me for two minutes to VIP; I got to show you something.'

I followed Deshawn to VIP even though I really didn't want to.

"So what is it? What is it you got to show me?" I crossed my arms.

"Look at her." He pointed back to Damiah. "Look at her right now. Does she looks like she gives a fuck about you?"

I turned back to Damiah and she was back at the bar with her friend. She was so chill. It was crazy to think that we were just seconds away from leaving the club to her acting like I wasn't even there. She didn't even care. It's like that whole shit with me and her never fucking happened. She wasn't even looking around for me at all. She was just normal.

"She's good. She not thinking about you." Deshawn was telling the truth because now she was drinking it up like I wasn't there. "You got to let this chick go. I get that she's a bad bitch, but she ain't worth the damn stress. You can't stay sprung off of this chick."

"Yeah," I replied, not really hearing what he said.

Usually when you leave a woman that is feeling you, she looks for you everywhere. She will be by your side because she wants to fuck too. Damiah is unbothered and doesn't give a fuck about me. Deshawn is right. I need to stop thinking about this bitch and go about my business. Back in VIP I saw the sexy chick with the thighs was back. She looked at me and smiled. Was I really about to throw away guaranteed pussy over Damiah? I was fucking crazy.

"Hey, it's my favorite customer." She walked over to me and gave me a hug. "I'm finally off of work."

"So that means you can have fun with me." I sat down in VIP.

"Yes, we can have all types of fun." She giggled. "What can I get you?"

"Nah babe, you are off the clock. Let these other people work for you." She laughed. "Come on, I got you."

"Nah Daddy, I got you." She smiled. "Don't worry about nothing tonight." She got up and headed to the bar. She came back with two bottles. I started to pull out money and she turned me down. "I told you that I got you."

This chick was so cool. She had this banging body and beautiful face. She had this sexy tongue ring. Every song that came on she danced on me like she was a talented ass stripper. Deshawn was smiling at me while he had two chicks on each side of him.

"Tell me that this is much better than before. Isn't this a better choice?" He was grinning like crazy.

"Way better choice." I laughed.

"Popping bottles…" He held up one of the bottles.

"And fucking bad bitches!" I yelled back at him.

"That's what the fuck I'm talking about."

The party kept going. I turned to the side and happened to see Damiah with her friend. She looked at me but then moved on. She didn't care.

"You okay?" Fatima asked holding my chin.

"I'm good," I replied back and she smiled. I leaned back so she could really dance on me. I had my hands on her thighs and she giggled then licked her lips. "Now let's get back to business."

CHAPTER 7

Damiah

"That club was dead!" I complained to Britanya as we got in her house. We just came back from the club. It was cool at first, but the whole thing turned out to be a dub.

"What are you talking about? That shit was lit." She rolled her eyes. "I would have love to stayed there all night...."

"What? At that dead ass place?" I sat on her couch. "Trust me, we'll have more fun if you and me just sit here and vibe out."

"I got some of that sticky if you want to light it up."

"What are you waiting for? Bring that shit out."

She went to go the bud and I got undressed. I found an old t-shirt of mine and some old shorts. Britanya's place was practically like my second house. I have extra clothes over here. In the bathroom, I let my long hair down and wiped the little makeup that I had off my face. I put on some of her face cream.

"Bitch, where you at?" Britanya yelled from the living room.

"Girl keep ya panties on, I'll be right there."

Britanya was in the living room already rolling up. She took off her club clothes and had on a sweatsuit. She looked at me up and down. She must have noticed me wearing my old clothes.

"Oh, I see you finally decided to get some of your shit." She laughed. "The way you leave shit here, I swear you think that my house is your house."

"Heifer, this is my house." I teased. "You know you sitting on my couch, right?" I laughed. "There goes my kitchen and there goes my TV."

"Then you need to pay your bills." We both started laughing. "Yo, what's going on with you?"

"Nothing." I shrugged my shoulders.

"Bitch, you already know I know you like the back of my fucking hand. You need to tell me what's up because I always find out."

Britanya was right. I just wasn't in a good mood tonight. I told her earlier today that I needed to get my mind off of things and I thought that going to the club that would do it, but it didn't work. My mind was still all fucked up.

"So what's going on with you?" she asked me again after she lit up the blunt. When the blunt stayed lit, she took three long pulls. "Tell me what's on your mind because you been on some shit lately." She blew some smoke out.

"Just bullshit as always." I reached out my hand for her to pass me some of that good stuff.

"Okay…"

"This whole thing with Shane is just making me mad," I admitted.

"Shane?" She shook her head. "Why didn't I think about that? It's always shit with Shane that gets you acting like this. Shane should have been my first guess."

"Yeah."

"So, what is it this time?"

"This time he is talking about his girl."

Shane has called this basic bitch his girl before but this time I think he really meant it. I think he really was trying to move on and be with this chick. Was he really feeling her? Was he falling in love with her? Was he going to marry her? WasIs he going to make her my son's stepmother? I couldn't have that bitch come in here and destroy everything that we had. She was trying to replace me, and that sad excuse of a woman couldn't do that. She would never be me and that's a fact.

"So what are you going to do? What are you thinking about?"

"I'm not even sure yet." I sighed. "But I can't let this bitch act like she's part of the family. I need to get this girl out of his life and mine. She is just driving me crazy."

"And how are you going to do that?"

"I am not sure."

"I mean if he's claiming her that must mean he likes her. He's not going to just let her go and she don't look like she's leaving."

"You don't have to remind me. I just want that bitch out of the way. She's seriously fucking up everything up for me. I don't know how I'm going to do it, but that basic bitch is going to be gone."

"Okay…" She inhaled it in and passed the blunt over to me.

I took a long pull and held the smoke in for a while. I needed this medicine. All this shit with Shane had me really stressed out. Him and this "girl" of his was really fucking my head up. I just didn't get how he could act like that I didn't matter.

"You know that nigga was really on the phone defending this bitch?" I told Brit. "He was like going in on how me and him are nothing but parents. Brit, this coming from the same nigga that was talking about marrying me and how he loved me. He can say that shit one day and then turn around and want to be with this bitch the next? He wants to act like I'm going crazy but he is the one that is going back on his word. Now I'm the bad guy? I'm the bitch because I want to make him a man of his word? He's the one that said those words and now I'm supposed to let that shit go? Fuck that shit."

My eyes started getting watery and I could feel the tears thinking about coming out. I wasn't going to let myself cry though. To be honest, I was sick and tired of always crying over this nigga Shane and the bullshit he was putting me through.

"I am just so over and done with this shit. I'm over it." Brit handed me back the weed. "Brit, he tells me loves me and that we are going to be together forever and now suddenly it's over? How can it be over after so long? He is the love of my life."

"I know," Brit added.

"And we met in high school and shit was all chill."

"I know that, I was there." She sighed.

"And now...nothing?"

"I don't know what to say." She rolled her eyes.

"What else is there to say? You know that we belong together. You know that right?"

"Listen, I know nothing, but this has been

going on for a long fucking time," she snapped. "It's all bullshit."

Looking at Brit, I could tell that she was over the conversation. She took a long pull from the weed and was still shaking her head.

"I'm sorry, did I say something to make you mad?"

"Girl, you know I love you and that I always got you back, but I wouldn't be your friend if I didn't keep it real with you. I can't just watch you do this shit. I got to be honest with you."

"And what is that?"

"You don't know what the fuck you want."

"I do. I want Shane."

"Oh yeah? And what about Trell?"

I blushed and smiled. I forget sometimes that I tell Britanya everything. Of course, after me and Trell fucked, I told her, but damn, I didn't think she would throw it back in my face.

"I don't know," I told her truthfully.

"See, that's what I'm talking about. You talking about you and Shane but you obviously feeling Trell too. I saw you guys earlier tonight at the club. You were all over him. You put his hands on your ass and that nigga was looking at you like you were a snack."

"It's not what it looks like."

"Why else would he have his hands on your ass? Was he trying to feel something?" She smirked and I gave her a look.

"I don't know." I was trying to play it off because I didn't want to admit to anything with Trell right now. I took another pull from the blunt. Brit was staring at me and I knew that she wasn't going to let this shit go. "I'm not going to lie to you. I do like Trell," I finally told her.

"I know, I can tell that, but I don't understand what you are doing. You can't be all about one of them and then mad at the other."

"Please, I've never been mad at Trell. I'm always going through some shit with Shane, I admit that, but not with Trell" I told her but she didn't look like she believe me. "I'm not mad at Trell."

"Really? Then why were you staring down that bitch that was with him tonight?"

"I wasn't looking at that ho."

"Please girl I saw the way you was eying that chick. You was getting a little mad."

"Whatever."

"And why did we suddenly leave? I was having a great time there. That whole shit was lit and out of nowhere you wanted to leave."

"Because the club was dead."

"The club wasn't dead Damiah, and you know that. No, we left because you couldn't stand seeing Trell with that woman."

I was about to argue, but Brit was kinda sorta right. I was looking at Trell and that chick all night. She just appeared out of nowhere and stayed on his lap all night. I would have thought that he would have looked for me or something, but he seemed fine with that chick. He was enjoying himself only minutes after he was all over my ass.

"What do you want Damiah? Who do you want?"

"I want my family."

"And what about Trell?"

"I don't know."

"You are adding fucking drama to your life, D. You need to make a choice between them. If you keep going the way you are, you are going to have more of a headache. You think shit is bad now, but imagine how it's going to be with two of them guys in your life. Imagine how it's going to be with that shit. You think you have drama now? You need to leave all that shit alone."

"How can I?"

"How? Make a fucking choice and stick with it!"

The blunt was done and I didn't even feel better. I got where Brit was coming from but how could she tell me how to live my life? She was no angel. She be bouncing from nigga to nigga and now she wanted to give me some speech. She never fell in love the way I did with Shane.

"I know what I'm doing, believe that. I'm going to get my man back and get my family back together. Once I finish doing all that, my life is going to be perfect."

"I hope so, girl. I love you and the last thing I want is for some fucking drama to go on with you. I just want you to be happy."

"And I will be once I get Shane back and get rid of that basic bitch Jayla. I'm going to get him back...one way or another."

CHAPTER 8

Jayla

"So, what is the reason you called me over here?" Shane and I were at this small little pastry shop. I have a little bit of a sweet tooth, but I wasn't in the mood to eat anything. I just wanted to get to the bottom of this. After the last conversation with Shane I was still confused. I really liked him, but this whole thing with his baby mother was going too far. Just how much was I supposed to take? Was I supposed to just forgive and forget? Or should I just move on and leave this all in my past?

"First and foremost, I want to thank you

for meeting up with me," he started but I shook my head.

"Don't start with that buttering me up thing. Please, just get straight to the point."

"I spoke with Damiah and everything is straightened out."

"Hmm, now where have I heard that before?"

"I know I've said it before but this time for sure she knows what it is. She's not going to bother you don't have to worry about her anymore. I'm sorry for all of this. I know that when we first met we promised to be open with each other and I was holding back. You told me from the beginning that you didn't want any drama and I feel like I brought you nothing but drama. I just want you to know that I really care about you and that I take us serious. I'm not going to let anyone come between us." He reached out and held my hands softly. "I just thought that you should know."

Hearing Shane tell me how he felt about me felt good, but hearing him defend our budding relationship felt great. He was all in and so was I.

"Thank you for that." I smiled. "I know that wasn't easy to do."

"But you're worth it," he assured me.

"So now what happens?"

"Now we focus on each other. You focus on me and I stay focused on you. Does that sound good?"

"That sounds great."

Ever since then Shane and I have really committed to each other. When he said he was taking us seriously, he really meant it. We made a promise that we would go out with each other at least three times a week. It didn't matter if it was dinner, or the movies, or even just hanging out at his house or mine, but we had to see each other. Tonight, we were going to a carnival. I hated carnivals and all that amusement park thing. Maybe because when I was a kid I never got to go. With my father gone and my mother on drugs, who would have time to take us kids to the amusement park? I think that's why Shane was so determined for us to go out there.

"Aw you look so cute." Crystal smiled, walking into my room. I was looking into the full-length mirror at my outfit. It was a cotton candy pink spaghetti strap dress with some white flats. My hair was pulled back in a pony-tail and I had on some diamond stud earrings that Shane gave me as a gift.

"Thank you." I sighed. "Shane told me he wanted me to dress fun like I was a kid."

"Aww that's so cute," she gushed. "Shane is the sweetest." She poked me. "And he makes you so happy."

"I know." I felt myself blushing.

"And I love what you've done over here." She was walking to a corner in my bedroom. "I think that's great."

In the corner of my room on top of my dresser was a bunch of things I kept from dates I went to with Shane. When we went to the movies, I kept the movie theater ticket stubs from the romantic movie I dragged him too. When we went to this bookstore I kept the small book that I bought. And for every date that we had, we took pictures and I actually went to get them printed and framed. It was nice to see the photos here instead of my phone. With the photo being out, I would always see the smile on my face when I was with Shane. In every picture, I looked so happy and that's how I felt; I am extremely happy.

At the carnival, I tried not to have fun, but Shane wasn't having it. As soon as we got there, he made us take the love tunnel ride. It was dark and filled with hearts and pictures of romantic couples. It was so nice and romantic, so I couldn't feel angry about my past anymore. After that, we went on a couple of rides. I am afraid of heights, but Shane held my hand and I did it. When we went on the Ferris wheel, I thought my heart was going to leap out of my mouth. I thought that I would pass out, but Shane was there making sure that I felt okay. He pushed me to do things, but he didn't make me feel scared.

"Okay, I know what's next," he said as we got to the food court. "We need to stuff our face like little kids." He smiled. "How about some cotton candy to go with that dress?" He laughed.

"Oh, ha ha." I faked laughed along. "You're so funny. Did anyone ever tell you that?"

"Yup, that's why my nickname is Kevin

Hart," he lied, winking at me. "But let's do that."

"We can't stuff our face with all this unhealthy food. Besides, you're the face of your gym, so you can't get fat."

"What are you talking about? If I get fat that will be perfect! Then I could lose the weight and say it was my gym that turned it all around," he joked.

"You're doing the most. "

We stuffed our faces with corndogs, cotton candy, and some soda. After we finished with that, we just walked around holding hands. We passed by this game where the prize was a huge stuffed zebra.

"I got to win that prize." I rushed over to the stand. "All I have to do is get three balls into the basket." I gave the worker some money.

"Let me get that for you." He threw down some more money.

"No it's okay; I think I can get this."

"How about we see who wins it first?"

"What does the winner get?" I asked.

"Hmm, how about the winner gets to watch the loser go on that ride?" He pointed to the tallest ride at the park. It was a straight drop from the top and it slowed down just a few feet off the floor.

"It's on, because there is no way in hell am I getting on this ride."

The contest started. Shane started throwing balls into the basket, but they kept bouncing out. He was getting mad and he kept paying the man over and over again. I just sat back and watched him because I had to figure out what I was going to do. If I lost the contest, I would die on that ride. The sign next to the ride said it was over 150 feet tall. My hands started shaking thinking about me on that ride. It was bad enough that it was so tall, but there was no seat. I would just be strapped on standing, waiting to meet Jesus.

"You're not going to try? You know that means that I win by default, don't you?"

"What?"

"The winner has to get the three balls into the basket." He smiled.

"Okay. I know that." I stepped up. "I was just watching you spend at least $100 on a stuffed animal that can't cost no more than $30."

"That's not the point. The point is to win." He was cheesing again. "Now don't punk out. After I win, I want to see you on that ride. I'm going to get a nice picture of your scared face." Shane was rubbing it in, but I couldn't give in to him.

"You talking a lot of shit for someone that hasn't gotten a ball in the basket yet," I reminded him.

"I'm just warming up." He laughed. "Now stop stalling and go."

I threw the first ball lightly and by a miracle it went in.

"Lucky shot." Shane chuckled. "I bet you can't do it again." I didn't answer, and I threw another light shot and it went in, too. "You cheating." He took one of the balls out of my hand and switched it with his. "I think they gave you better balls or something."

"Don't be mad because you don't know how to handle your balls." I laughed.

"Bet you can't make the last shot though." He stopped and waited for me to do it. I took a deep breath and threw another light throw. Once again, the ball went in.

"Yes!" I jumped up and down. I started

dancing right next to Shane. "What was that mess you were talking about?"

After a lot of us going back and forth, he had to take it like man. He went on the ride and tried to sit on the far side so I couldn't see him. I followed him though and took out my phone.

"Smile for the 'Gram," I teased. "I'm putting this all over the Internet, so try not to pee on yourself."

"Man," he said, trying to sound confident, but when the ride went up, I saw the fear take over his face. I couldn't see much of him when he was all the way at the top. When I spotted him again, I waved, but I doubt he could see me. When the ride dropped him, my heart dropped too. When the ride was over, he walked over to me.

"How was it?"

"It wasn't bad." He smirked. I put my hand on his chest and felt that his heart was about to go crazy.

"Your heart is saying otherwise." I laughed.

"It's only doing that because I saw you." He grinned.

"You think you're so smooth."

When we arrived at my house, I noticed that Keon's car wasn't here. I looked at my phone and I saw that I had a missed call and a voicemail. I listed to the message and Keon was letting me know that he was taking Crystal away for the day.

"Hmm." I hummed after ending the call.

"What's wrong?"

"My brother and his girl isn't home."

"Oh."

"You want to come inside and just hang out?"

"I would like that a lot."

I poured myself a drink and asked Shane if he wanted anything. He requested a soda and I sat next to him, sippin' on my white wine.

"So, did you have fun today?" He looked straight into my eyes.

"I have to admit it that I did. Thank you for this."

"Not a problem; besides, I like spending time with you."

"Oh yeah." I put my drink down and took

his soda out of his hand. "How about you show me?"

We instantly kissed each other. He grabbed me close and I sat on top of him. He put his hands on my ass and squeezed. I bit his neck down hard and he moaned out loud. I knew he loved and hated when I did that to him. Sometimes when we were in public, I would grab and kiss him and then bite his neck. He would laugh and say that I didn't know what I was doing, but of course I did. I loved messing around with him like that.

He held my face and kissed my lips softly.

"Damn, I just love your lips," he whispered. "I can kiss them all day." He bit my bottom lip and then went on to kiss my neck. He bit down softly and then softly pecked all over. We then started to lay down on the couch just making out. It was getting hot and intense. I just wanted him so badly, but I didn't give in. Usually by this point, I would be trying to rip off his clothes, but this was enough right now. Him on top of me, touching me everywhere, making me want him...was enough.

We made out for what felt like hours and

eventually he had to go. We were at the door just hugging each other and holding on to each other. It felt so good to be in his arms and for everything to not be about sex all the time. Him holding me felt great and as I held on to him, I could feel it coming out of me. I could feel the words being stuck at my throat. I felt myself about to tell him that I loved him. The words lumped up in my throat and it felt like I was choking on it. I wanted to say it out loud, but I didn't think I was ready to say it out loud yet. But as I kept trying to stop myself from saying it, the more it felt like coming out. So while I hugged him tightly, I mouthed the words "I love you," and I felt better.

"I can't wait to see you again." He was still holding on to me tightly.

"Well in order for that to happen you would have to let me go," I joked.

"You say that like I'm the only one holding on." We let each other go at the same time. He kissed my lips and then my forehead. "I'll call you when I get home."

Weeks went by and the dates kept getting better and better. We started to do more than just go on dinner dates. Now we went to paint and wine parties, sailing on a boat, cooking classes, comedy shows, and we tried to meet each other for runs in the morning. During the past few weeks, I hadn't heard or even seen Damiah. Shane was right. Not only did he take care of it, but he managed to make the dates even better. I felt closer and closer to him. I was falling for him and it was scary, but for the most part it felt nice.

Monday back to work use to be a drag but when every Sunday was a brunch date with me and Shane, the next day was great. I got to work and everybody was staring at me. By the time I got to Samara, I was starting to be suspicious. She was cheesing at me looking at me up and down.

"What is going on?" I asked, looking around. "Why is everyone looking at me like I got something on me?" I looked at myself. My scrubs were clean and everything. "And why you cheesing too?"

"Oh maybe it's because what's for you at the front desk." She took my hand and led me to the front. "You need to stop coming in by the back door."

"But that's where I parked my car. Samara, what's going on?"

She didn't answer me but instead brought me to the front desk. The desk was covered with vases filled with long stem roses. There was so many roses in all colors that it looked like a mini garden.

"And don't even ask because all of them are for you." She smiled. "My brother is really going all out for you." I still was in shock as the receptionist handed me the card.

"I couldn't decide which one to get you, so I bought them all. You make me so happy and I hope that this can show you that. I can't wait to see you again." And the note was from Shane.

"So, you know…." Samara came up to me. "I never did get a thank you for hooking you up with my brother. He's got you smiling and glowing and everything. I should really get a thank you."

"Thanks Samara, but I'm pretty sure I have told you before."

"You know what will work. Maybe if you give me some of these roses." She smiled.

"Now, you're doing too much."

"Oh come on. He makes you happy and I

know he really is feeling you. The least you could do is give me one rose. I mean you are falling in love with him and everything."

"Fine, whatever." I laughed and started to get ready for work. I didn't want to tell her that I had already fallen for Shane...at least not yet.

Trell

My head was spinning and I felt myself leaning but I still grabbed the rest of the bottle of vodka. I was so fucked up, but I needed this. I was trying not to think about everything that was happening but then it all came back to me. I was in my office going over all of the paperwork. Throughout the years I got information on Shane. I had a nagging feeling about him for a while but now I actually had a chance to do something about it.

I hired some guys to follow around Shane and now I knew his every move. The papers had all his movements that he made every day.

The folder was filled with pictures of the places that he went to and even had some of him and that new chick Damiah was talking about. Now it was time to put my plan to action.

I know for sure Shane is the reason why I got locked up. It was a gut feeling I had. I was suspicious that this nigga was shady but I let shit slide. When we were out making moves, I could see that he was doing things differently. Back in the day, he did what I said with no questions asked, but now he was always trying to do things for himself. He kept complaining about making money through drugs. He was trying to go legit, but I told him that was crazy.

"I'm just saying, you need someone to watch the business and have clean hands. I should step away for a little bit and focus on that," Shane told me one day while we were sitting at the diner.

"What the fuck are you talking about? Me and you are running this shit. We are making all the moves and making sure that shit gets done. There is no walking away for this! It's either we die or we go to jail, that's it!

Everyone thinks that they can just go legit or some shit, but you can't. Even if you did stop and do that shit, do you think that your past just disappear? Your hands are dirty no matter what you do."

After having that conversation with him, I should have stopped the whole situation. I should have taken care of him then, but I didn't. He was my right-hand man so it was hard to see him being grimy, but now I knew better. When I was in prison it was like I was still outside because I just kept getting information. People kept telling me about the things that were going on that I couldn't see. I kept hearing whispers that Shane was why I was in prison. Once I saw how much money he was making and how he was opening all the businesses, I knew it was him. He was going to go legit no matter what I said or did. I guess he thought that if he got me out of the way it could be more possible.

I opened up the folder with all the documents. One of the pictures that I saw was Shane hanging out in front of this rundown building. It was him and three other people. I noticed the "For Sale" sign. Maybe he was looking at the building to start another gym. He thought he was so smart but he was not.

Shane fucked up when he didn't check up on me. He just locked me up and walked away. He just thought that he could live his life and that was it. He never thought to check up on me so he could see where my head was at. He could see if I felt bitter or anything. He didn't see me as a threat and that was his big mistake. He didn't take me seriously, but once I took care of him, he'd know. He'd know not to fuck with me. Once he died, everything would be fine.

I was planning Shane's death since in prison and the second that I got out, I was putting my plan into motion. At first, I was just going to run up on him, but that would have been sloppy. I would have gotten caught and went back to prison. Since I didn't want to be locked up again, I had to be smarter. When I got the guys to follow him around, I made sure they did it for months. I wanted to know every move and be able to predict his habits. If he had a favorite place to eat, I wanted to know. If he like to go to the movies, I wanted to know that. There was nowhere that Shane could go to without me knowing. Now that I had all this information it was time for Shane to die.

The gun in my hand felt right. Finally, after all this time, Shane was going to pay for all that he had done. He was going to be dead and everyone around him would, too. Me and Karma were going to take care of that bitch ass nigga.

∾

FIND out what happens next in His Dirty Secret Book 10! Available Now!

FOLLOW Mia Black on Instagram for more updates: @authormiablack